It's Mine!

By Janine Amos and Annabel Spenceley
Consultant Rachael Underwood

A CHERRYTREE BOOK

This edition first published in 2007
by Cherrytree Books, part of
The Evans Publishing Group
2A Portman Mansions
Chiltern Street
London
W1U 6NR

Printed in China

British Library Cataloguing in Publication Data.
Amos, Janine
  It's mine!. - (Good friends)
  1. Sharing - Pictorial works - Juvenile fiction
  2. Children's stories - Pictorial works
  I. Title II. Spenceley, Annabel III. Underwood, Rachael
  823.9'14[J]

ISBN 184234417X
13 digit ISBN 978 1842344170

CREDITS
Editor: Louise John
Designer: D.R.ink
Photography: Gareth Boden
Production: Jenny Mulvanny
Based on the original edition of It's Mine! published in 1999

With thanks to our models:
The treasure map
Yim Poonsen, Rena Jutla and Louise John
The tiger mask
Edward Higgins, Alex Evans and Lewis Robertson

VISIT OUR WEBSITE
www.evansbooks.co.uk
Evans

The Treasure Map

Everyone is making treasure maps. There is one piece of gold paper left.

"It's mine!"
says Rena.
"I want it!"
says Yim.

"We can both use it,"
Rena tells her.
Rena starts to work at
one end of the paper.

Yim agrees.
She works at
the other end.

They make the treasure map together.

"It looks great," thinks Yim.

"It's finished!
I'll put it on my
bedroom wall,"
says Rena.

"I want it on my bedroom wall!" says Yim.

How do you think Yim feels?

"I've got an idea,"
Miss Johnson tells them.
"Would you like to hear it?"

"One of you could take it home today. The other can take it home tomorrow."

"Yes, let's take it in turns!" says Rena.

"Who'll go first?" wonders Yim.
"You can!" offers Rena.

At hometime, Yim rolls up the map carefully.

"Thanks, Rena," she says. "Tomorrow it's your turn!"

The Tiger Mask

Lewis comes to play at Edward's house.

Edward has a
new mask.
It is a tiger mask.

Edward puts it on
and growls.
"Grr!"

Edward paces around the room like a tiger. "Grr! Grr!"

Edward pulls away

"I want it!"
says Lewis.
He grabs the
mask.

Edward pulls away.
"It's mine!" he shouts.

Lewis pulls and
Edward pulls.

The mask gets broken.

Edward starts
to cry.

Edward's mum comes over. "Oh, it's broken," she says. "What can we do?"

"We can fix it. We can stick it back together," says Lewis.

Edward gets
the sticky tape.
Together they
fix the mask.

Now Edward is a tiger again.

And Lewis has found a giraffe mask to play with.

TEACHER'S NOTES

By reading these books with young children and inviting them to answer the questions posed in the text, the children can actively work towards aspects of the PSHE and Citizenship curriculum.

Develop confidence and responsibility and making the most of their abilities by
• recognising what they like and dislike, what is fair and unfair and what is right and wrong
• to share their opinions on things that matter to them and explain their views
• to recognise, name and deal with their feelings in a positive way

Develop good relationships and respecting the differences between people
• to recognise how their behaviour affects others
• to listen to other people and play and work co-operatively
• to identify and respect the difference and similarities between people

By using some simple follow up and extension activities, children can also work towards

Citizenship KS1
• to recognise choices that they can make and recognise the difference between right and wrong
• to realise that people and living things have needs, and that they have a responsibility to meet them
• that family and friends should care for each other

EXTENSION ACTIVITY
Discussion – responsibility and fairness
• Sit the children on the mat with a flipchart at child height and read the first story – *The Treasure Map*. As you go along ask the children questions about the text to check that they have understood. At the end of the story ask the children what they think Rena did that was good/fair.
• Write the word Fair at the top of the flipchart and draw a line down the centre of the page. Place a tick on one side and a cross on the other. Point out to the children that sometimes it can be hard to be fair and sometimes it can be easy. Using the tick side, ask the children to think of times it was really easy to be fair and why, e.g. 'because there were lots of sweets to go around' and list them. Then ask them to identify times when it was difficult to be fair, e.g. 'because he called me names and I didn't want to be kind to him'.
• Explain the importance of fairness to the children and that fairness is a choice. Here are some questions you can ask to stimulate the children's thoughts:
Do you think Rena found it hard to be fair?
What might have happened if Mrs Johnson hadn't come along?
Do you think the end of the story was fair?

These activities can be repeated on subsequent days using the other story in the book or with other stories in the series.